Treasure
in the
Toilet

PHASE 5

/ie/eal/

Level 8 – Purple

Helpful Hints for Reading at Home

The graphemes (written letters) and phonemes (units of sound) used throughout this series are aligned with Letters and Sounds. This offers a consistent approach to learning whether reading at home or in the classroom.

HERE IS A LIST OF ALTERNATIVE PRONUNCIATIONS OF GRAPHEMES FOR THIS PHASE OF LEARNING. AN EXAMPLE OF THE PRONUNCIATION CAN BE FOUND IN BRACKETS.

Phase 5 Alternative Pronunciations of Graphemes			
a (hat, what)	e (bed, she)	i (fin, find)	o (hot, so)
u (but, unit)	c (cat, cent)	g (got, giant)	ow (cow, blow)
ie (tied, field)	ea (eat, bread)	er (farmer, herb)	ch (chin, school, chef)
y (yes, by, very, gym)	ou (out, shoulder, could, you)	o_e (home)	u_e (rule)

HERE ARE SOME WORDS WHICH YOUR CHILD MAY FIND TRICKY.

Phase 5 Tricky Words			
oh	their	people	Mr
Mrs	looked	called	asked
could			

GPC focus: /ie/ea/

TOP TIPS FOR HELPING YOUR CHILD TO READ:

• Allow children time to break down unfamiliar words into units of sound and then encourage children to string these sounds together to create the word.

• Encourage your child to point out any focus phonics when they are used.

• Read through the book more than once to grow confidence.

• Ask simple questions about the text to assess understanding.

• Encourage children to use illustrations as prompts.

PHASE 5

/ie/ea/

This book focuses on the phonemes /ie/ and /ea/ and is a purple level 8 book band.

Treasure
in the
Toilet

Written by
John Wood

Illustrated by
Marcus Gray

Mr Grumpton was teaching art. There were paints and models everywhere. Just then, Deepa burst into the room.

"Mr Grumpton, Mr Grumpton," she said.

"Archie has a problem... in the toilet."

When Mr Grumpton got to the toilets, Archie was standing outside. He looked dazed. They went inside.

The room was bathed in a golden glow.
Mr Grumpton peered into the toilet. There,
in the water, he saw something shimmering.
It was a poo. The poo was made of gold.

"You did this, Archie?" asked Mr Grumpton, his mouth hanging open. He did not believe it. "Yes, Mr Grumpton," said Archie, with a proud smile.

Mr Grumpton wiped the sweat from his forehead.

"This is bad," he said. "Have you told anyone else?"

Archie shook his head.

"Good," said Mr Grumpton. "If anyone finds out about this, they will come after you, Archie. They will catch you and use your golden poo to get rich. Scientists will do tests on you."

Just then, there was a loud knock on the door.
"Who's in there?" said a voice outside.
"Don't panic," said Mr Grumpton.
Archie panicked. He dreaded the idea of
scientists doing all sorts of tests on him.

Mr Grumpton cracked the door open. It was
Cathie the caretaker.
"Archie is not feeling well," Mr Grumpton said.
"Well... I'll be back," Cathie growled.

"That was close," said Archie. Then he flushed the toilet.
"No!" shouted Mr Grumpton.

There were clangs and bangs as the poo was sucked through the pipes. As the poo left, the sound got quieter and quieter until the bathroom was silent.

"Someone is going to find that poo," said Mr Grumpton. "We have to get out of here!"

They left the bathroom and went down the corridor. But Cathie was behind them! Mr Grumpton and Archie ran ahead, but Cathie ran faster.

Mr Grumpton tipped over a box of pencils. They rolled everywhere. As Cathie stood on the pencils, she slipped. She fell on her bum with a loud THUMP. Mr Grumpton and Archie ran around the corner.

They ran into the headteacher.

"Ah, hello," said the headteacher. "Mr Grumpton, I need to speak to you. There is a spelling quiz that I think you need to give the children..."

The headteacher talked and talked. Mr Grumpton tapped his foot. Time was running out!

Mr Grumpton pushed the headteacher into the art closet and locked her in.

"She is going to be so mad with you," said Archie.
"That is the last thing I am thinking about," said Mr Grumpton.

There were lots of black cars outside.
A woman was waiting for them.
"We have been told that a golden poo came from here," she said.
"Run, Archie!" yelled Mr Grumpton.

Lots of people were chasing them.
"It is the boy who can poo gold," said one
of them into an earpiece. "Don't let him get
away."

"Quick," said Mr Grumpton. "We can run through the flowerbeds!"

"But we aren't allowed on the flowerbeds," said Archie.

"Run through the flowerbeds, Archie!" yelled Mr Grumpton, as he trampled the headteacher's petunias.

Archie was out of breath. Just then, a man appeared.
"You and your golden poos are going to make me rich," he said.

"Quick!" said Mr Grumpton. "We can get onto the roof!"

"But we aren't allowed on the roof," said Archie.

"Get onto the roof, Archie!" yelled Mr Grumpton, as he bumped into the caretaker's bins. Pieces of rubbish flew everywhere.

But Cathie the caretaker was on the roof.
"I cannot believe it," said Mr Grumpton.
"I am going to sell your poos, Archie!"
shrieked Cathie.

Just then, Deepa burst outside. She had a big bag of golden poos and she threw them onto the field. Everyone ran on the grass and scooped up all the poos.

Mr Grumpton and Archie came down from the roof and hid in the bushes with Deepa.

"The poos are not real," said Deepa. "I got everyone in art to make them while you were away! We used clay and gold paint."
"That was clever, Deepa," said Mr Grumpton. "Good job. This will give us a chance to get away."

"Quick, get in," said Mr Grumpton.
"What am I going to do, Mr Grumpton?"
said Archie, as they flew away.

"Well, you can't stay here," said Mr Grumpton.
"I'm taking you home. You and your mum and
dad are going to start a new life in the North
Pole!"
"OK," said Archie. "But can we stop on the
way? I need the toilet."
"Not again..." said Mr Grumpton, feeling
afraid.

Treasure in the Toilet

1. What was Archie's poo made of?

2. How did Mr Grumpton get the headteacher to stop talking?

3. Who was waiting on the roof?

   a. The headteacher

   b. A scientist

   c. Cathie the caretaker

4. What do Archie and Mr Grumpton fly away in?

5. Would you like to start a new life in the North Pole? If not, where would you go to start a new life?

©2021 **BookLife Publishing Ltd.**
King's Lynn, Norfolk PE30 4LS

ISBN 978-1-83927-423-7

Treasure in the Toilet
Written by John Wood
Illustrated by Marcus Gray

An Introduction to BookLife Readers...

Our Readers have been specifically created in line with the London Institute of Education's approach to book banding and are phonetically decodable and ordered to support each phase of Letters and Sounds.

Each book has been created to provide the best possible reading and learning experience. Our aim is to share our love of books with children, providing both emerging readers and prolific page-turners with beautiful books that are guaranteed to provoke interest and learning, regardless of ability.

BOOK BAND GRADED using the Institute of Education's approach to levelling.

PHONETICALLY DECODABLE supporting each phase of Letters and Sounds.

EXERCISES AND QUESTIONS to offer reinforcement and to ascertain comprehension.

BEAUTIFULLY ILLUSTRATED to inspire and provoke engagement, providing a variety of styles for the reader to enjoy whilst reading through the series.

AUTHOR INSIGHT: JOHN WOOD

An incredibly creative and talented author, John Wood has written about 60 books for BookLife Publishing. Born in Warwickshire, he graduated with a BA in English Literature and English Language from De Montfort University. During his studies, he learned about literature, styles of language, linguistic relativism, and psycholinguistics, which is the study of the effects of language on the brain. Thanks to his learnings, John successfully uses words that captivate and resonate with children and that will be sure to make them retain information. His stories are entertaining, memorable, and extremely fun to read.

PHASE 5
/ie/ea/

This book focuses on the phonemes /ie/ and /ea/ and is a purple level 8 book band.